Go with Your Heart

Savannah J. Frierson

SJF
BOOKS

Go with Your Heart

Copyright © 2016, 2010 by Savannah J. Frierson

Book editing/formatting by Savannah Frierson

Cover Art by Savannah Frierson
Image by jlutgendorf/Bigstock.com

ISBN-13: 978-1530627646
ISBN-10: 1530627648

Printed in the United States of America
by CreateSpace Independent Publishing Platform

To those striking out to fulfill their dreams and to those who help them get there.

Once Again

April 1870—Choctaw Territory
(Present-day Oklahoma)

"Come on up here, Shiloh! You promised us a song!"

Shiloh frowned, shaking her head as she wiped down the counter with Mary and Clarice chuckling under their breaths. The entire saloon started applauding, the patrons stomping their feet and whistling in support of the performance Shiloh had little desire to give. She wasn't the entertainer in their family; her brothers were. She was the one who made sure folks didn't have too much fun. It was expensive as hell to ship inventory into Liberton, with the town being in Indian Territory and All-Black to boot. They'd already had to replace three tables, seven chairs, and two cases of glasses from the brawl three weeks ago—not to mention the precious alcohol wasted. They still hadn't fully restocked on the bourbon. Just like men to choose Washing

Day as the day to lose their everlovin' minds. She'd barred the perpetrators from coming back until they'd managed to ingratiate themselves into her good graces.

Which was why *they* were currently doing the laundry on *this* Washing Day.

"Go on, now; you know this racket's gonna keep up until you do," Mary said, grinning at her husband when he winked in her direction. Clarice giggled beside her and nodded.

"It'd be nice to hear something melodious for a change too!" her other coworker added.

She glared mildly at them both. Just because they were married to her brothers and had become the sisters she'd never thought she'd have didn't mean she had to cater to their whims! But Clarice's father had been the saloon's previous owner and Mary's mother, though not in full support of such a "den of iniquity", did drive the men who stayed at her boarding house here for business. And then there was the fact she really did love to sing.

Just not in front of a bunch of drunken people!

Yet the cheers grew louder and more obnoxious, so she finally heaved a sigh, threw down her wiping rag, and went up to the small dais where her oldest younger brother, Albert, sat at the piano and her baby brother, Philip, sat with the banjo in his lap. Philip even had the audacity to wink at her as he handed her the clapping spoons she would need to perform.

"You love us, Sis!" Albert reminded her, beginning to play the strands of an old song from their plantation in Vicksburg.

"You lucky because of that, you know," she muttered under her breath, but her responding wink had him throwing back his head and beginning the verse.

For the next thirty minutes they played, Shiloh making sure not to get too lost in the music so she could keep an eye on things. Every once in a while Mary or Clarice would nod to her in reassurance, and she'd shimmy her shoulders to let them know she understood the message. It was a bit freeing in that regard, that she could stop and start a task because she felt like it, not being ordered around, demanded, or commanded as someone's property. Sometimes she still pinched herself that she was here, her own woman, instead of working in the fields alongside her brothers and grandfather. In fact, it had been Pa Lou who'd convinced their master's son to take her when he'd handpicked her brothers to go to war with him. "Ain't nobody else gon' keep 'em in line, suh," he'd said. "An' she-a gud warsherwoman too."

She honestly hadn't wanted to go, too worried about who would take care of her grandfather without her there. Her mother had died giving birth to Philip and her father had been beaten and sold back east to Georgia or Carolina for daring to protect her from a lusty slave driver. It was only because Pa Lou had been such a loyal servant that the master had allowed the family one final goodbye.

"Y'all mind your sister, you hear?" the broken man had wheezed to his young sons. Shiloh had been thirteen, but she'd felt older than Pa Lou then. She'd felt guilty, too, for her papa had taken the punishment really due to her. She'd been the one who'd almost castrated the slave driver—just as papa had taught her to do should some man try to force himself upon her. And then she'd kicked him good in the eye just to make sure he'd known she'd meant business. The only reason Papa hadn't died was because the slave driver had broken one of the master's rules—the slaves weren't to be touched. The master had thought it unholy to lie with those not of one's kind.

Shiloh shook her head to free herself of such morose ponderings. The crowd in the Gilded Canary was raucous with approval, especially at Philip's spirited banjo solo. Shiloh played her spoons like Pa Lou had taught her while Albert tickled the keys. They harmonized on the last few bars of the song before Philip finished with a flourish on the banjo. Shiloh nodded her head instead of doing elaborate bows like her brothers, which enabled her to keep an eye on the bar.

The arrival was a newcomer. They'd been working at the Canary for almost four years and pretty much knew the regulars; he was not one. Shiloh didn't know if he was new, period, or just to the colored part of town. The Canary didn't turn away anyone willing to spend an honest coin, but Shiloh could admit they didn't get a lot of patrons who weren't colored. But he wasn't creating any problems so far, so Shiloh relaxed just a little.

"So, when you gon' let me court you, Shiloh?" came a deep voice from behind her.

She arched an eyebrow and smirked before turning around to meet the voice's owner. She placed her hands on her hips and blinked once at him. "As soon as your wife turns into a widow!"

The patrons around her laughed, and the man who'd spoken, Tony Coombs, scowled at them good-naturedly. "Aw, you know Kimmy would love for you to take me off her hands!"

"She shoulda had better plannin' when she married you then—I ain't nearly that charitable!" Shiloh returned.

The crowd laughed again, including Tony, who tossed a silver piece at her with a wink. She nodded her thanks and went back to one of her safe havens in the saloon—the bar. The newcomer didn't glance up at her arrival, which was just as well. It gave her the opportunity to scope him out unguardedly.

She couldn't see his facial features. His hat, beaten and frayed at the brim, obscured the view. Long, straight dark hair draped broad shoulders clothed under a worn flannel shirt. The hands around the cloudy, yet clean mug were cracked, blistered around the knuckles, and bruised; but they were strong hands, full of life. Shiloh wasn't sure if their burnished gold color was from the sun or something natural. He could be a breed.

"First time here," she said. It wasn't a question. The man nodded but didn't provide details. "Hope you found everything okay." Another nod. Clarice and Mary looked to her for more cues but she shook her head, indicating for them to leave him in peace. He wasn't creating any problems and all money was good money. They would be foolish to turn down business.

Other customers came and went as the evening wore on, but their silent newcomer remained in place, steadily putting more coins on the counter to top up his drink. Which was lemonade. He drank it like it was going out of style, making him even more intriguing to Shiloh. Not to say Mary didn't make the best lemonade this side of the Mississippi, but it was rarely the beverage of choice at the Canary.

Voices began rising and Shiloh immediately went on alert. She palmed her five-shot Tranter that was tucked at the small of her back, but luckily Philip was there to stop the fight before it even began. It was obviously time to shut down the bar.

The men began their bellyaching but Shiloh remained unmoved. Mary and Clarice were also anxious to close down, judging by the heated looks they shot their husbands. Throughout it all, their newcomer remained seated, nursing his lemonade, as if he were determined to be the last patron out.

She ran her fingers over the barrel of the revolver again. Though she preferred knives, guns provided more chances to get it right, and Mary and Clarice knew how to use one as well.

"Y'all go on," she told Albert, who was reluctantly hanging back with his wife to walk Shiloh to the boarding house where she lived. Mary's mother still thought she needed a chaperone even though she was twenty-four—an old spinster to most men now—and worked in a saloon. Not that Shiloh would ever admit it aloud, but she didn't mind the care so much. It'd been almost twenty years since she'd been mothered.

The man didn't move, though he must've felt the look of death her brother had shot him as he and Mary left hand in hand. It was dark save for the lamps behind the bar. Shadows fell across them both as he continued sipping on the lemonade and she wiped down the rest of the bar. She didn't feel uncomfortable or even threatened by her companion, but she didn't know what to say to him, either, so she kept silent. He didn't seem the type for idle chatter; which worked for her, since she didn't speak unless she had something to say. So they remained in mildly uncomfortable silence until he finally drained his glass.

Finally! she thought, and reached out to take the glass when his hand suddenly clamped around hers. In a second her revolver was out and the barrel was against his temple. It was only by providence she didn't squeeze the trigger.

"Very good, *Kana.* I see you have been practicing."

The gun would've clattered to the ground if the not-quite-a-stranger had had poorer reflexes. The man lifted his head then, black eyes piercing and so familiar. Full lips curved to a smirk while the hand clamped around her eased its grip to caress the bones of her wrist as it slid away. He tossed the gun in the air to get a firmer hold on the gun's barrel, then he gave the weapon back to her butt first. She took the gun, her dark-brown eyes still wide with shock and something else she had no desire to investigate at that moment, only hoping he couldn't see it.

"Nashoba," she whispered.

"*Halito, Shiloh, chim achukma?*"

She smirked a little as she tucked the gun back into the small of her back. "I'm fine, Nashoba. Better than the last time we saw each other. How are you?"

"A," he said, nodding for emphasis. "It is good to see you and your brothers are doing well for yourselves."

She arched an eyebrow. "You've yet to answer my question."

His smirk settled into a genuine grin and he lightly chuckled. "Sharp and astute as ever, *Kana*. I am alive. I suppose I am to interpret that as a blessing."

"A, *Kana*," she replied in his native Choctaw. "It is always good to know a friend is still around." To that end, she took some of the silver pieces out of the lockbox she'd just secured and handed them to him. "You don't ever have to pay for anything here."

He shook his head. "That is bad business, *Kana*."

"We wouldn't have this business if not for you," she insisted, wincing at the earnestness in her voice.

Nashoba eyed the silver, glanced at her, then pushed it back to her. "Whenever else I come in, I will not pay. You earned this money, so you should keep it. Knowing you and your brothers are doing well is payment enough."

She sighed a little but returned the money and put the lockbox back. "Fine."

"And the fact you still call me friend is also payment," he added, his grin growing larger.

Shiloh bit her lip to keep her smile from growing. "You started it."

Nashoba chuckled again. "<u>A</u>, that is so."

Shiloh turned to douse the rest of the lights, so many questions whirring through her mind. It had been six years since she'd seen him, since he'd guided her and her brothers to a Union camp under moonlight. She hadn't wanted to leave him in the midst of war, with the deafening reports of guns and the smell of smoke and burning flesh. She'd tried in vain to convince him to stay with them. But he'd smiled, kissed her forehead, and promised he'd always be with her. Shiloh didn't know how that would've been possible when neither she nor her brothers had any idea where they were going after their escape; but they'd ended up West, and West was a lot of territory. Still, that hadn't stopped her heart from beating extra fast whenever she'd caught a glimpse of someone who could've been familiar. Funny how it remained steady when she finally did reunite with the man who'd changed her life so much.

Shiloh heard him stand and she glanced his way as she moved from behind the counter to the door. He approached but maintained space between them. She'd forgotten how tall he actually was, having to tilt her head way back to look into his eyes. Then again, her brothers weren't tiny, either, but it was merely a cock of the head to look at either of them. The lamps from the street provided a little light in the otherwise darkened saloon, but she wouldn't have needed that to know he was staring at her. The power of his eyes couldn't be ignored.

"I will walk you home," he said softly.

She shook her head and left the saloon, his footfalls thumping behind her on the plank steps. "That's unnecessary. It's just down the way, within shoutin' distance."

"Your brother thought it fit to walk you there before he left."

"I'm a single woman and he thinks I can't take care of myself," Shiloh said, walking on to the boarding house. Nashoba's laugh curled into her ears, making her smile.

"You know that is not true. He just wants to make sure you do not have to, *chilita ohoyo*. That is what one does for someone he holds dear."

Shiloh looked away from him to hide a blush he wouldn't be able to see even if it were high noon. Very rarely did someone speak to her with unadorned tenderness. Nashoba had called her brave and was still able to acknowledge the fact she was a woman. Even her brothers could be borderline crude with her, but that was their way. She didn't put up with foolishness or posturing, but that didn't mean the feminine part of her didn't want or appreciate soft words and gentle phrases. Granted, she preferred britches to the long skirts most women wore. She enjoyed the freedom and the ease with which she could move. She also thought that much fabric was a bit wasteful, and she didn't abide by unnecessary excess.

"It is the same reason why I am walking you back, Shiloh. That and because..."

He didn't continue, as if letting the memories of what happened between them all those years ago swirl around them. It had been intense, bringing about irrevocable changes for her, she knew; but she sensed for him as well. Definitely for his people. She couldn't help but hear of the battles going on throughout the territories between the Indians and the Army. But he was here, and at least the shell of him was whole.

"I've missed you too," she whispered, stealing a peek at him.

"Hmm," he intoned, stroking his chin. "*Miha moma...*"

Shiloh burst out laughing and shoved him lightly. "I will *not* say that again! You lucky you got that much out of me."

"I have gotten more than that in the past."

She abruptly stopped walking; luckily for her, they were at the boarding house now. He turned to her, his lips tilted in a half grin. Shiloh looked down at her feet to hide her responding smile, the boots she wore dusty from the road and scuffed from age. A larger pair of boots, much newer and nicer, came into view, the tips of those touching the tips of hers.

"I will see you again," Nashoba said.

"In another six years?"

"Not quite that long," the deep voice replied. "Sleep well, *Chunkash Champuli.*"

Sweetheart. Grinning wider, Shiloh kept her head bowed and didn't raise it again until she was sure Nashoba was out of sight. She spun to her left and walked up the steps into the boardinghouse. Mary's mother, Karen, was dosing in the chair near the window, no doubt staked there so she could see when Shiloh arrived.

"Miss Karen?"

The heavyset woman shot up, eyes wide and darting around until they finally fell upon Shiloh. Mary was practically the spitting image of the woman, only Mary wasn't nearly as intimidating as her mother—at least not to her. She was sure Albert had a different opinion on the matter, however.

"Lord, have mercy! Gave me a fright!" Karen scolded, then she chuckled. "Tried to wait up for you."

"You didn't have to, Miss Karen."

"Girl, if you don't stop calling me that! Mama Kay! I ain't even fifteen years older than you, and I'm your mother-in-law too!" she insisted, framing Shiloh's face in her hands and shaking it. The slight frown she wore deepened. "But I think I need backup—must find you a husband!"

Shiloh shook her head and patted Mama Kay's hands, backing away from the maternal woman. "I'm not really inclined to trade one version of bondage for another, Mama Kay."

Mama Kay scowled now. "You think Mary considers her union with Albert bondage?"

Shiloh sighed, undoing the braided chignon at her nape and combing out the strands with her fingers. Her hair fell like a black cloud about her shoulders. "No, ma'am. But it's different for them. Philip and Clarice too. They're young and without baggage. I'm not. The only men interested in me are those who are desperate."

"These here are desperate times," Mama Kay said, following Shiloh upstairs into her room. At the moment it was just she, Mama Kay, and the live-in maintenance man, Mr. Upton, who were staying here; but the last boarder hadn't left a week ago yet. Shiloh was sure a new one would be arriving any day now. "And you *really* need to think about settling down!" the older woman added, eyeing the bed pointedly.

Shiloh approached the bed and sat down gently so not to disturb it. Her hand rested upon a small, brown forehead before smoothing back dark curls and she sighed. A single woman with a child but without the protection of a husband could face many dangers, whether that woman knew her way around a fight or not. Shiloh also didn't want her daughter to scratch and claw the way she'd done. Though she'd come into the world during Shiloh's very first snowstorm, at least the child had been born free. Shiloh couldn't think of a better start than that.

She bent her head when Mama Kay squeezed her shoulder and whispered goodnight. Shiloh returned the goodbye and changed into a very frilly nightgown Clarice had made for her last birthday. It was very comfortable, and her daughter loved playing with the sky-blue ribbon at the bodice. She eased into bed next to her child, who immediately snuggled into her. Smiling gently, Shiloh kissed the top of her daughter's head and stared at the wall until her memories coaxed her into slumber.

Like the First Time

She always kept her head down while she did the laundry, which made Nashoba that much more eager to see what she looked like. He didn't think he'd be displeased, considering her form was enough to have the men's tongues wagging about the Negress at the laundry. She was always surrounded, either by the other washerwomen or her brothers at the end of the day, and they never let her out of their sight. Nashoba didn't blame them. Generally, the slaves remained tight together anyway, and any liaisons between the slave women and the soldiers took place away from the main camp.

For himself, Nashoba didn't want to be here, and he definitely didn't want to be wearing this scratchy gray uniform, either; but it was his duty to his Nation to serve. He'd been working at the Office of Indian Affairs in Washington when the War started. Negotiations and positioning really intensified then between the governments and the Nation, but the Confederacy won, to Nashoba's expectations. They'd been winning the war, and it was to the Nation's best interest to align with whomever would be the victor. And as much as he empathized with the Negroes and their plight, he had his own people to consider first and foremost.

That hadn't meant he'd leapt at the opportunity to enter the fray. He'd tried his hardest to remain at his post in Washington. Nashoba didn't see why the Choctaw or any of the other Nations should get heavily involved in the White Man's Fight. As the Nations knew, they spoke with forked tongues, and a promise today could be a betrayal tomorrow. But when his mother had sent him a message saying his aging father was going to fight for their family, he'd sent a response back as fast as he could, saying he would take Shikopa's place.

That had been a year ago. Now he was here in a Confederate camp with the strange status of hero for helping to rescue other soldiers from a train wreck. Nashoba didn't particularly trust this goodwill to last very long, but he was not *hatak hopoyuksa*, a foolish man. He would accept it as long as it was given.

"You are staring again, Brother," came a tease in Choctaw.

Nashoba smirked and raised an eyebrow, but didn't turn to his friend-turned-brother in battle. "It cannot be helped."

Koi chuckled behind him, his black hair held at the nape of his neck by a string of leather. He was barefoot, saying he'd rather touch the cold ground than shove his feet in too-tight shoes. They weren't allowed to wear moccasins. Nashoba's shoes were a bit better, having needed to wear European shoes to fit in with Washington Bureaucracy, but he also preferred no shoes when in the privacy of his quarters.

As if feeling the power of his gaze, the woman glanced up and met his eyes. The stirring of the clothes in the vat slowed while his heart rate increased. Her face was round, as were her eyes, with skin the color of a tree trunk but as smooth as water. He wanted her to smile so she would confirm it would be as lovely as he imagined going by the shape of her mouth with its plump lips; yet, there was really no reason to smile while doing the task she was doing in her current circumstances. But that just meant he now had two personal missions other than the one mandated to him by the Confederacy.

To learn her name and her smile.

She dropped her eyes and returned to her work. Koi tugged Nashoba into the tent they shared, but his mind never strayed far from the beautiful laundress. For the next week, he made it a point to meet eyes with her, but her expression remained unreadable. Koi and his other brethren made him the butt of many jokes, but they didn't bother him. He was a patient man.

He was also very lucky dinner was even less fulfilling than it normally was one night, so he decided to return to his tent earlier than most of the other men did. Meals were usually the times when everyone would relax and talk, but Nashoba preferred quiet this night. He was walking down his tent row when he spotted her entering his tent with a basket of wash in her arms. The other washerwomen of their company were entering and exiting more tents, so he hastened his steps to make sure he caught her before she left.

She was placing neatly folded clothes upon their bedrolls, straightening up stray items that could pose tripping risks to her as she completed her tasks. The ragged edges of her long skirt swept against the ground as she moved, creating a soft brushing sound in the otherwise quiet dwelling. He stood straight with his hands at his back, trying to think of something to say; but sooner than he'd anticipated, she turned around and froze, her eyes widening.

Nashoba cleared his throat and stood even taller. "Hello."

She blinked, shrank back slightly, then nodded and mumbled a greeting in reply. Her body went rigid when he came closer, so he went to Koi's side of the tent and drew parallel with her. She shifted so her back was mostly to him, as if one wrong move from him would have her pivoting for quick flight. Nashoba kept his movements slow as he knelt down and took off his shoes, grinning a little when he noticed her watching him out the corner of her eye.

"My name is Nathan," he said, using his white name. She nodded but remained silent. Maybe she was forbidden to talk to the soldiers. Yet he recalled the other washerwomen talking to the men in camp, so he dismissed that theory.

She stood from her slight stoop, gave him one more nod, and started for the exit. In a split-second decision,

Nashoba blocked her, and her eyes widened, her gasp more deafening than a cannon's report just then. He shook his head, his hands splayed wide in a gesture of peace. Wary eyes stared at his hands, and he grasped his wrists behind his back.

"I mean you no harm," he assured her. "I would only like to know your name. Please."

"Did I do something wrong?" she asked. Her voice was a melodious alto, its tone very pleasing to his ears.

"Nothing at all. I wish to thank you," he explained. "For the laundry."

"You don't need my name to do that," she told him, staring at the ground.

Her wit made him grin. "This is true. I thought it would be more personable if I used it, however."

"Unnecessary. I'm merely doin' my job." She started forward again, and this time he moved so she could pass. He poked his head out of the tent to follow her with his eyes. She didn't look back. That only made him more determined in his quest.

For the next two weeks, every morning on the way to breakfast and every evening from dinner he would greet her.

Initially, she wouldn't even glance up from whatever she was doing—washing, mending, or flat-out ignoring him. But eventually, he would get a soft, one-word reply.

She still wouldn't look at him, though.

Instead of growing frustrated, he counted every breakthrough as a small victory. His brief interactions with her made his entire experience at camp worth it. Though regarded as heroes for saving soldiers' lives, he and the other Choctaw soldiers still weren't deemed fit to truly fight. They were used to keep the few prisoners of war and slaves in line, and all were getting annoyed and resentful of the indignity. They'd trained for a year to serve in a war that wasn't even theirs; Nashoba was afraid noncombat action would give the Confederacy a convenient loophole to further renege on treaty promises. As it were, the Nations had barely received any of the aid they'd been promised, and winters in the Territories were much harsher than in Mississippi.

"I don't know if I want us to win or them," Koi said during one dinner. His tablemates nodded, understanding the indecision. Nashoba picked over his hardtack, wishing he had his bow and arrow for some old-fashioned hunting. This gruel wasn't fit for a gnat, let alone a grown man. After another fifteen minutes of pretending to eat something, he and his brethren left to return to their tents; but strains of music diverted them from their original destination. They all followed it, the strains of a banjo, fiddle, voices, and clapping rising up from an unidentified location. A few moments later they spotted the crowd, white soldiers making a semicircle around a group of slaves. Nashoba's breath caught when he recognized one of the singers as his Laundress. She was clacking a set of spoons on her thigh and smiling widely at one of her brothers who was dancing while playing the fiddle. The other strummed the banjo and stomped his foot to keep time, providing vocalizations to aid in the song. Some of the soldiers started dancing around the fire; but as soon as one tried to get close to his Laundress, banjo-playing brother would stare him down while fiddling brother jigged in front of her.

Nashoba decided then and there he liked them.

"I understand the staring now," Koi said from beside him. Nashoba didn't take his eyes away from her, but he did nod. "She is very pleasing to the eye."

"Her smile is like sunrise," Nashoba determined. He visibly started when her eyes locked to his, and her bright smile slipped. His heart clenched at that reaction before beating faster than ever before when the smile returned, though far softer and shyer than it had been for her brothers and fellow performers.

Sa-yukpa, he thought to himself. *My smile.*

He remained until the music ended, though the crowd had begun to thin over an hour ago. He smiled when she gave her brothers large hugs, rubbing the younger one's head with affection. Unable to stop himself, he approached them, her brothers immediately going on alert and scowling fiercely at him.

"Yes?" the older one said.

Nashoba blinked. He'd thought the older one was actually of age, but his voice hadn't completely dropped yet. When the brothers fully grew, they would probably rival him in height, if not in weight. The youngest one was at his sister's chin and the elder one was slightly taller. That didn't mean they wouldn't fight him to defend her.

"I just wanted to say I enjoyed the performance. You all are very talented," he praised, making sure to meet each of their eyes. His lingered on hers, and she looked away shyly.

They nodded, but he didn't leave. Neither did they. Both parties, instead, observed the other. The silence stretched on until his Laundress cleared her throat and placed her hands on her brothers' shoulders. "This is Nathan; he has been kind to me."

"How kind?" the older one asked, crossing his arms at his chest.

His Laundress laughed lightly. "He actually said please."

The younger one's eyes went wide. "Really?! Nevah had a white man say please before!"

Nashoba internally winced. He knew his appearance enabled him easy passage between two worlds, especially since he'd worked for the American government, but he was not ashamed to be Choctaw. Nevertheless, it wouldn't be wise to correct the young one, at least not yet.

His Laundress bit her bottom lip and gave a short nod. It seemed she would keep the truth to herself too. "Well, he did. And now I will thank him for the kindness he showed me. Thank you, sir."

"You are welcome..."

"Shiloh. And this is Albert and Philip," she added, indicating the elder and younger brother respectively.

"Nice to meet you," he said, smiling, especially because he finally got her name and her smile.

"We must go. Again, thank you for your compliment and your kindness."

"You are welcome, Shiloh...Albert, Philip."

She ushered her younger brothers toward their section of the camp, but this time she turned back and looked at him. And smiled.

Nashoba wasn't entirely certain he hadn't floated back to his tent. Koi looked up from the carving he was doing and smirked.

"Finally talked to her?" he asked.

"<u>A</u>," Nashoba replied. "Her name is Shiloh."

Nashoba would be eternally grateful the Confederate commanders had thought so little of their battalion, or else they would've been sent to Vicksburg to die. Instead, they were commanded to help protect Meridian, mainly patrolling the railroads or the city itself. They would occasionally do some scouting to make sure they weren't ripe for an ambush too.

Because patrols could be tedious at times, Nashoba had started carving to pass the time. At first, he'd had no thought of what he wanted to create, but a shape began to take form of a flower. He knew then it was to be a gift for Shiloh. He hoped she would accept it.

She'd begun greeting him first now whenever they met. Even her brothers would say hello. At some point, she and other slaves—both men and women—were assigned to aid in building fortifications or hauling supplies in Meridian. Nashoba knew the Spirits were looking favorably upon him because he was assigned to escort her supply wagon to and from town. They exchanged smiles as he helped her up onto the seat to drive the wagon.

"You probably shouldn't have done that," she told him once she was settled, picking up the reins.

"What has been done cannot be undone."

They didn't speak on the ride there, but Nashoba enjoyed the private concert she gave as she sang under her breath. When she lapsed, he would hum songs his father used to sing. They would share mutual grins while not looking at each other.

Nashoba spent the day patrolling while Shiloh made the deliveries. At the end of the day, Shiloh drove the wagon back full of the day's workers that had walked to the town. Both still didn't speak to each other, but they did enjoy the stories their passengers told about their day. When they arrived back at camp, Nashoba helped her take care of the horses and the wagons. He watched her bond with the geldings as she fed them.

"You like animals," he noted, coming up to stroke one of the geldings' faces along with her.

"They are nice. Loyal. You take care of them and they love you in return."

He moved behind her as they kept stroking the horse. Her body tensed a fraction, but then relaxed. He didn't touch her, but he did bend down to speak into her ear.

"It can work that way with humans too."

She didn't immediately reply, her hand dropping from the horse. He continued to stroke while she went to the other gelding. "Reckon that's what a Ma and Pa do—take care of they chiren and then we love 'em in return."

"Exactly," he said.

"And that's what these white men expectin' from us," Shiloh added, some grit in her tone now.

Nashoba scoffed. "Arrogance is a man's downfall."

"You fight for them," she reminded him. "Y'all think like them, even though they don't like you much, either."

"Not all of us do," Nashoba cautioned her. "Just like all white men don't believe in bondage."

She peered at him, wrapping her thin shawl around her shoulders to brace against the temperature that had dropped considerably since that afternoon. "Just not enough of you, I suppose."

Unfortunately, Nashoba couldn't argue that point. "You trust I'm not one, though."

Shiloh shrugged. "I trust...you'd be kind to me."

Nashoba frowned briefly before he reared back as if her very words burned him. He felt offended and ashamed all at once. She wasn't merely responding to him, but actually offering herself to him. Should he desire, she'd be willing to be his paramour until...when? He died in battle? The war ended? She escaped? It was a pragmatic choice, a single woman with two younger brothers at the mercy of men who might not be as kind as he was. His jaw clenched at the necessity of such a gambit.

"Did I misread your intentions?" she asked softly.

"Misconstrued," he amended, approaching her before she could flee around him. "I will, however, offer my protection to you—"

"The girls told me there's a creek about a half a mile from here where—"

He shook his head fiercely, pressing his thumb against her lips to silence her. "I will teach you how to protect yourself so you'll never have to do this again."

She tilted her chin up and he dropped his hand. "You are the first."

He spoke clearly, his eyes starkly focused upon her. He fisted his hands at the small of his back. "And I will be the last you'll ever offer yourself to in such a manner."

Next Steps

May 1870—Choctaw Territory

(Present-day Oklahoma)

The sermon that Sunday morning had been as dry as the cracked earth they walked on the way home. Five-year-old Tempest had been antsy all throughout the service, alternating between the laps of her aunts before Mama Kay had popped one chubby thigh and trapped her onto her lap for the rest of the sermon.

Tempest rode on Uncle Philip's shoulders as they sang the songs from the service. That had been the best part of the whole morning for her, and Shiloh was inclined to agree. Sometimes it was hard being on the choir stand with her daughter out in the congregation without her, but she trusted her sisters-in-law, and nobody could make a child toe the line quite like Mama Kay.

"Mama, can we have chicken for dinner tonight?" Tempest asked, leaning over her uncle's head to whisper in her mother's ear.

"We're eating at Aunt Clarice and Uncle Philip's tonight; what we have for dinner is up to them," Shiloh informed. Truthfully, anything they'd eaten since the war was a step up, but thankfully Tempest didn't have that period with which to compare anything. She'd scrounge up chicken for the rest of her life if it meant her daughter never knew the chains of slavery.

"Chicken? We were thinking of ham—"

"Ham!" Tempest squealed, thus interrupting her aunt. "I love ham!" The adults laughed at the child's excitement, Shiloh allowing her daughter to nuzzle her tiny nose against hers.

Tempest did her best to help her mother, Mama Kay, and aunts prepare dinner, but she soon became too inquisitive and had to go into the living area with her uncles and watch them play checkers. Occasionally, Shiloh would poke her head in and see Tempest either in one uncle's lap or the other, a small, thoughtful frown on her face as if she were going over strategy on their behalf. Shiloh chuckled at her daughter's precociousness and only prayed it would remain endearing when she became older.

"I was just saying, Shiloh, that new doctor was looking mighty fine," Clarice said, bumping Shiloh with her shoulder. "You saw him, right? Sitting next to us?"

She made an uncommitted grunt, but of course the other women took that as a resounding yes.

"He was really sweet to Tempest, also. Gave her a peppermint. I know you saw *that!*" Mary added with a grin.

Pursing her lips, Shiloh nodded curtly, her attention on the chicken she was battering in the flour mixture Clarice had prepared. The grease in the cast-iron pan sizzled and popped, ready for frying, but she felt she was about to go in there instead of the raw meat she held!

"And then he came up to you and said you sounded like an angel. I almost melted in a puddle. He has a deep voice, Shiloh. Very nice smile. Clean. You need to set your feather in *that* cap, let me tell you!" Mama Kay declared, and the other two women nodded.

Shiloh heaved a deep sigh and bowed her head. "You invited him to dinner, didn't you?"

"Even better—I invited him to *board!*" Mama Kay revealed.

Shiloh resisted tossing the chicken in the pan with her annoyance. The doctor had been in Liberton a week, word of his arrival reaching the Gilded Canary almost as soon as he'd stepped foot into town. Seemingly seconds after that, so had he. He was from back east, judging by the way everything on him appeared new. He'd looked around the Canary as if he were reacquainting himself with a familiar place. Shiloh had flashed him a welcoming smile; but the way his returning smile had created unease in her belly had had Shiloh hiding in the glasses that had suddenly needed re-cleaning.

"Now you'll have to say more than two words to him!" Mary cheered.

"I can't wait for school to start back up," Shiloh muttered, placing another piece of floured chicken into the frying pan. Mary was actually the town's schoolteacher; but since classes were out for the farming season, she worked at the Canary. While there, Mary seemed to spend as much time scoping out prospective husbands for Shiloh as she did serving drinks. Every order Mary took involved an interrogation of age, employment, and marital status of a new patron.

Clarice and Mama Kay thankfully left the kitchen to set the table, and Shiloh managed to ignore Mary's plans of wedded bliss for her and the new doctor. Lamont Clinton was a perfectly all right fellow—handsome, mannerly, smart, kind. After he left the bar with his gin and hello to her, he would sit with the sheriff and other townsmen to debate the news of the day. He had an opinion on everything—the rebuilding in the South, the expansion into the Territories, Indians. He'd smoke his pipe as he spoke, nod silently if he agreed with a point or tap his pipe when he didn't. She winced to herself that she knew those facts, but it was her job to observe people, after all.

She'd also "observed" Nashoba not coming into the Canary since that night, which had been almost two weeks ago. Though he'd said he'd see her again, that hadn't necessarily meant the next day, obviously. She had no idea what he did. Maybe he worked for the government again; maybe he'd just been passing through. Shiloh shook her head and flipped over the chicken pieces to fry on the other side. Maybe it was time to tuck him back into the tiny corner of her heart reserved for him.

Dinner was ready in another hour. When Clarice walked out with a platter of golden fried chicken, Shiloh had to scoop up her daughter to prevent her from knocking over the woman with her joy.

"Chicken! Chicken!" she exclaimed, bouncing up and down in the chair where Shiloh had deposited her.

"Do not move or touch," Shiloh said.

"Yes, Mama," Tempest replied, but her eyes were locked upon the chicken in anticipation.

Shiloh was bringing out the corn when she heard the knock on the door, and cursed when she bobbled the bowl a little. All that earlier talking in the kitchen made her nervous, which made her scowl at the corn. She had no reason to be. She wasn't trying to impress him, anyway.

"You ready?!" Mary asked, coming in to get the cornbread from the oven. That was the last of the food that needed to be brought to the table. The mashed potatoes and gravy was already out there with the green beans.

"Yes, let's get this started," Shiloh muttered and followed behind her sister in law.

Of course the only empty seat left was beside Dr. Clinton. Tempest, the turncoat, sat between her uncles, clapping joyously for the food she was about to receive. Mama Kay and Clarice's father Orville sat at the heads of the table and her sisters-in-law were seated on the other side of her. Everyone held hands while Mr. Orville said grace, Shiloh making sure to squeeze the pulse out of Mary's hand for setting her up like this. Mary's gasp of pain during the "Amens" brought a satisfied smirk to Shiloh's face.

She didn't say much during the meal. Then again, few outside of Dr. Clinton, Mama Kay, and Mary did. Sometimes Tempest would interject with a question or comment of her own, usually totally unrelated to the current topic. But to Dr. Clinton's credit, he would acknowledge her daughter with patience and a smile, so she couldn't completely put knocks against him. He also tried to ask Shiloh direct questions, but Mama Kay or Mary would beat her to the answer. It'd gotten to the point Dr. Clinton just asked them outright, which was fine with Shiloh.

She wasn't one for small talk.

Sweet potato pie was for dessert, which made Tempest and her uncles happier than cats with cream. Afterward, Shiloh was the first one up to begin clearing the table, and the three women immediately crowded her in the kitchen.

"So! What do you think?"

"I think he's a winner!"

"He's got manners, was real nice to Tempest, and gainfully employed! You really can't do better, Shiloh!"

She took measured breaths before answering. "I really have little interest in a husband—"

"And yet it's in your best interest *to* have one—especially little Tempest's!" Mama Kay hissed. "That's one man who isn't desperate and I really think he'll be good to you and your baby."

"Now, I think you might get further if you didn't work at the saloon—"

Shiloh cut off the rest of Mary's comment with a glare. "The only person in this kitchen who *doesn't* work at the Canary is Mama Kay, so, please, *do* be hypocritical!"

"Our husbands are there," Clarice said with a shrug. "And it was my father's before he sold it to y'all. But it's different when you're the wife of a doctor. Those are different expectations, Shiloh."

She groaned. One family dinner with the man and he was suddenly her husband!

Because dusk had already set and Tempest's bedtime was soon, she and Mama Kay decided to leave early. Albert and Mary chose to visit a little longer. Shiloh was forgiving enough to accept Mary's kiss to her cheek, but she still sent one parting glare before she left.

Mr. Orville flanked Mama Kay's left while Dr. Clinton flanked Shiloh's right. The older couple set the pace for the stroll to the boarding house, and Shiloh raised her eyebrow at how close they were to each other. Tempest sagged against her mother's leg as she walked, and Shiloh chuckled at her daughter's energy finally being depleted.

"I can carry her, if that is your wish," Dr. Clinton offered when she lifted her daughter onto her hip. Tempest immediately curled around her and began to sleep.

"No, thank you," Shiloh said, smoothing down her daughter's curls. "I'm fine."

"She's a little big to—"

"This isn't the first time I've had to carry her by myself, Dr. Clinton. I did it for almost a year and no man could've helped me then."

She heard his amusement in his chuckle. "That is an unusual and clever way to describe being with child."

"Oh, Shiloh is *full* of cleverness, yes!" Mama Kay trilled, looking over her shoulder at him. "She has a quick mind, as you can see!"

"Yes, I do," Dr. Clinton agreed, his eyes sweeping slowly over her. "As quick as she is beautiful."

Shiloh hid her face in her daughter's hair as she adjusted her hold on her child. Tempest curled tighter into her mother's solid form. Thankfully, they reached the boardinghouse with little flirting the rest of the way. In fact, Dr. Clinton seemed content to enjoy the walk silently. She didn't know if that were for her benefit or Tempest's, but she appreciated the consideration nonetheless. She'd just stepped on the porch when Dr. Clinton called her name. Mama Kay took Tempest and offered to put her to bed so they could talk more.

"I won't be long," Dr. Clinton promised. "I'd like to walk Mr. Graham back to his home."

Mr. Graham wasn't so old as to need an escort right back down the street, not even in his fifties yet, but Shiloh suspected Orville wouldn't mind the company.

"All right," Shiloh agreed. "You want me to get y'all something to drink?"

"I don't think I need to drink anything else tonight. Need to rest these old bones, though."

Shiloh and Dr. Clinton shared a smile. Orville was as hearty as ever and they all knew it. Riding on the goodness flowing between them, Dr. Clinton stepped right up to the border of her personal space and inclined his head. "I was wondering if I may call on you later this week."

"I work all week," she said instantly, jumping a bit when there was a knock on the wall behind her. Of course Mama Kay would be right in her easy chair eavesdropping through the open window. Shiloh barely contained the urge to roll her eyes.

"I could walk you home, then?" Dr. Clinton tried.

"Every night?"

"That's my wish," he said, grinning a little. "But up to you. I'd like to get to know you, Shiloh. You're intriguing."

She arched an eyebrow and crossed her arms at her chest. "I choose to take that as a compliment."

"Good. I have no intention of causing you offense."

Shiloh looked off and bit her lower lip. She definitely appreciated quick wit too. It meant a man used his mind. Considering he was a doctor, she would hope so.

"Tomorrow won't be a good day for me. I have house calls to make. But Tuesday? Would that be okay?"

Between Shiloh practically hearing Mama Kay's bated breath and Mr. Orville nodding behind Dr. Clinton's back, Shiloh knew she could only answer affirmatively. The "Yes!" and clap heard from the open window behind her made Shiloh blush and Dr. Clinton's eyes sparkle.

"My sentiments exactly, Mrs. Lane!" Dr. Clinton announced. Mama Kay gasped and shut the window with a resounding thud. Even Shiloh couldn't refrain from laughing at that.

She remained on the porch until the men were out of earshot, then she went back inside. Silencing Mama Kay with a look, she kissed the older woman's forehead and climbed up the stairs to her bedroom. Tempest sat up bleary-eyed when she entered and smiled.

"We had fried chicken today!" she cheered, somehow finding a second wind. "They tricked me!"

Laughing lightly, Shiloh kissed her daughter's nose. "That they did. Was it good?"

"Yes, Mama, but I like yours better," she said, scrunching up her face.

"Now, don't tell Aunt Clarice that."

Wide-eyed, Tempest shook her head. "No, Mama, I won't!"

Still chuckling, Shiloh sat on the bed and Tempest immediately began undoing her chignon. She let her daughter play in her hair as she took off her dress and shoes. She didn't bother putting on a nightgown, the shift she wore under her dress making that unnecessary. When she lay down, Tempest giggled and climb right atop her, resting her cheek on her mother's chest.

"Is that man gonna be my new papa?"

Tempest could cut right to the heart of it when she wanted. Sighing, Shiloh smoothed down Tempest's hair and shrugged. "Do you want a papa, Tempest?"

Tiny shoulders shrugged. "I don't know. Mama Kay says I need one. Did you have a papa, Mama?"

Shiloh closed her eyes to the memories of her father's broken body, her last memory ever of him. But even that couldn't stop her from remembering, especially when he'd managed a small smile and nod for her. He'd protected her from a fate worse than death because of his love for her. Maybe it would be good for Tempest to have a papa who'd do the same for her. But was that man Dr. Clinton?

"I did. He was a good papa. You deserve a good papa, Tempest."

"Okay. I love you, Mama," Tempest declared, rearing up to kiss her jaw.

Shiloh kissed the top of her daughter's head and squeezed her close. "I love you, too, darling."

It didn't take long for Tempest to go back to sleep, but Shiloh's thoughts were too heavy for her to do the same. She wondered about the sudden anxiousness Mama Kay had. Her daughter had only been married for two years and Clarice only one, but maybe she felt an obligation to Shiloh also. There were more folks coming into Liberton, the formerly enslaved and migrants to work in the coal mines and the railroad; maybe Mama Kay was merely excited about the new prospects and the interest would die down once they'd been here for a while. Not only that, Shiloh liked being her own woman, making her own rules. Her daughter would know how to be independent, which was an invaluable asset. A Black woman's security was fleeting; she had to know how to maintain it or regain it if necessary.

At some point she fell asleep; for when she came to again, the sky was lightening with the promise of a new day. Suddenly antsy, Shiloh eased out of bed, wanting to steal the quiet of the morning for herself before getting ready to go to the saloon. She shoved her feet in some shoes and threw on a hand-me-down blue wool robe from Mama Kay, tucking her Tranter in the robe's sleeves. With one last glance to her slumbering child, she snuck out of the house. Even Mr. Upton wasn't awake yet.

She kept her ears open for any abnormal sounds, her revolver at the ready. It was utterly silent, Liberton still in bed for the most part this predawn Monday morning. She began walking toward the nearby creek; she would take a quick dip and rinse before returning to the house.

When she broke through the band of trees she realized someone else had beaten her there. The person swam with sure strokes through the water, barely disturbing it. She couldn't help but watch and admire. She wasn't nearly so graceful when she swam, but her papa had been determined she'd know how...just in case. Those lessons had certainly come in handy later on in her life.

"Hello."

She started, the voice pulling her from her memories. She stood straighter and stepped back when she finally met the eyes of the person she'd been observing.

"I'm sorry..."

"I don't mind," Nashoba said, walking closer to the creek's bank. "It seems we have the same idea."

She nodded, but continued going backwards. "I didn't mean to disturb you. I shall go—"

"Please stay," Nashoba requested. He looked off to the east. "The day is about to begin. I would like your company to welcome it."

She too looked eastward, the sky pinkening with the sun's rays. Making a decision, Shiloh took off her robe and her shoes and approached the bank. She noticed a pair of pants a few feet away and she raised her eyebrow.

"You're naked," she said.

He nodded. "Wanted to bathe."

So did she. Shiloh glared at him when he began smiling. "Oh, shut up!"

"I didn't say a word. It isn't as if you are a mystery to me, Shiloh, or I to you."

She huffed out a breath. "Fine, then." She refused to let him have the upper hand. Not looking at him, she whipped off her shift, shuddering a bit as the cool morning air hit her flesh. She still averted her eyes from him when she entered the water, and she didn't feel his traveling up and down her body in a way male eyes usually did while she was at the saloon. That fact compelled her to regard him, his gaze waiting for hers. And when he held out his hands to her, she had no thought of doing anything but placing hers in them.

Been Here Before

The past few months had been tremendously difficult. The heat was nearly oppressive, made worse by the stench of unclean bodies and death. Reports from other front lines weren't good, including the fall of Vicksburg to the Union forces. The Confederacy was now essentially split into two. Their camp had received an influx of Confederate troops, mainly released prisoners of the Union Army, Nashoba would find out from one of them, and some families of soldiers from new enlistees. He didn't think the Union general had done that out of the kindness of his heart, but rather from lack of resources. Either way, Nashoba figured the War that was supposed to be short in duration would just continue to drag on.

It was early in the camp, though there were some men already up and about. Most were headed to the creek for a wash and swim before drills began. For himself, he headed to the slave section, a section that had become increasingly more integrated with the amount of families arriving and the slaves escaping. He found Shiloh already up and bent over a tarp she was mending.

"Good morning, Shiloh."

"Morning, Nathan. Did you rest well?" she asked, glancing briefly at him with a smile.

"As well as expected. Yourself?"

She shrugged. "I think I managed an hour of uninterrupted sleep. Al and Phil, however, were logs. As usual."

He smiled and touched her shoulder. "Would you go on a walk with me?"

She bit her lip, her mending slowing until it stopped altogether. "All right."

He assisted her to her feet, then tucked her hand in the crook of his elbow. By now, the entire camp was under the impression Shiloh was his, especially considering he'd gone to her master and asked if he could personally protect his property. The boy had smirked but said yes, apparently trusting Nashoba wouldn't cause too much damage to one of his father's slaves.

They spoke little on this stroll, heading to an area of the creek that wasn't heavily occupied from the rest of the camp. When they found a good spot, they both stripped down—Nashoba to a loincloth and Shiloh to her shift.

"Let's see how well you'll do today," Nashoba said, tossing a branch the size of a small knife to her. She caught it and flipped it a few times, rising to the balls of her feet.

"Let's," she replied, then immediately went on the attack.

It was an invigorating spar, Shiloh taking the upper hand more often than she had the last practice. She was gaining in speed and strength, never staying down for more than mere moments before she freed herself and went on the offensive again. Nashoba wished they had real weapons, but they couldn't risk serious and unexplained injury. Never mind Koi still looked askance at mysterious bruises on his person, but he'd long stopped asking about them.

Suddenly, Nashoba was on his back, the wind ripped from his lungs, and staring at the beautifully triumphant face of his pupil.

"Finally!" she congratulated herself, then swallowed a yelp when Nashoba flipped them until she was on the ground and he was above her, his arms protecting her from the dewy earth.

"Premature declarations of victory are to be avoided, *Chilita*. They can leave you vulnerable."

"Oh, poot, you just know how to rain on someone's parade!" she said with a scowl, slapping his shoulder.

Smiling softly, Nashoba smoothed his thumb across her furrowed brows and stood, bringing her with him. She ended up hovering over the ground and grasped his neck with both arms.

"I won't drop you, Shiloh."

"You better not," she mumbled, but eased her hold. "But can you put me down?"

"When I'm ready, *Chilita*," Nashoba promised, and began walking them to the creek. She wrapped her legs around his waist for added security and looked over her shoulder so she could see where they were going. She gasped.

"The creek?"

"We are dirty. We should bathe."

"Together?"

Nashoba shrugged. "I am not ashamed of my body, Shiloh. And I can certainly suspect I will not be ashamed of yours."

Her eyes widened, then she buried her face into his neck and laughed. Nashoba joined her, running his hand along her back as he set her feet down on the ground.

"Well, I can say I'm not ashamed of yours, either, Nashoba. You are quite fit."

He quirked his eyebrows and took off his loincloth. Without waiting for her reaction, Nashoba rushed into the creek, then yowled at how cold it was. Shiloh's guffaws had him glowering at her playfully, but then he beckoned her with his hand.

"Do you dare, *Kana?*"

"*Kana?* You've never called me that before," she said, putting her hands on her hips.

"I have," Nashoba insisted. "*Kana* is friend."

Her mouth formed a perfect "O", then she cocked her head. "Does Nashoba mean Nathan, then?"

He grinned and shook his head. He'd told her his true name back when they'd initially started five months ago.

During this time, they'd learned much about each other. He'd told her about going to school at an Indian school in Kentucky then to a college where they allowed anyone to attend. She'd been surprised there were Negroes who weren't slaves, and who actually could go to school. He'd asked if she knew how to read and she'd admitted she could read very little. She recognized words more than anything else. He was helping her with that as well.

"Nashoba means wolf in Choctaw," he said.

She mulled over that information, tapping her chin with an index finger, then nodded. "I think it suits."

"Glad you approve."

"I don't know what my name means," Shiloh said. "I just know it comes from the Bible."

"That'll be our next project—to search for your name's meaning," Nashoba promised.

"Oh, goody!" Shiloh cheered with a clap.

"And you're stalling." Nashoba crossed his arms over his chest. "Are you going to bathe, or will you remain stinky-stinky?"

Shiloh gasped, then narrowed her eyes at him. "Humph! Turn around, Nashoba. I won't be on display!"

He chuckled, rolling his eyes at her show of modesty, but did as commanded. He walked further into the creek to see how deep it went. The water line hit his waist before he decided he'd gone far enough for now. He'd come back and investigate further.

"You can turn around now," came a quiet voice from almost directly behind him.

Shiloh was hugging herself, hiding her bare chest, when he did so. Nashoba kept his attention on her face and nodded his approval.

"Very good, Shiloh," he praised. "This is not so bad."

She grinned and shook her head, but she didn't drop her arms. "It's not very deep."

"It does not seem so."

"Okay." She sank into the water, getting low enough to hide her chest. Nashoba went onto his knees as well and leaned forward.

"We probably should have brought soap," he said conspiratorially.

She laughed. "Probably, but this is still refreshing." Her eyes fell to his collarbone, and he looked down to see a streak of red. "Sorry about that," she murmured, cupping her hand and pouring water over the wound. His hand pressed her palm against his flesh, and she regarded him with surprise.

"Never apologize for protecting yourself, Shiloh. Your life is the most cherished thing you possess."

She raised her eyebrows and stared at him for a long while. Then she trembled. Nashoba came closer and kissed the back of the hand he held. "Nashoba..."

He turned her hand around and grazed his lips against the pulse in her wrist. It settled him even more. He wasn't antsy despite them being in a war zone. He could be called to the front lines, never to return; but as long as she lived, he would be all right with whatever destiny he owned.

"You look at me like...like I'm somethin' wonderful," she whispered, then ducked her head.

Nashoba kissed the top of her head, placing the hand he held onto his chest while his free arm wrapped around her waist. They hugged, the nude form of her so soft and pliant against the hard form of him. There was nothing sexual in this embrace.

"Thank you for being kind to me," she said after some time had lapsed.

It was more than kindness on his part. That initial attraction and fascination had deepened, become far more profound than he'd anticipated. She'd become elemental to him, someone who required his utmost care. Her brothers had also become special to him. He was instructing Albert on how to carve a recorder while Philip had become a welcome shadow, soaking up whatever wisdom of manhood Nashoba chose to impart. He'd even asked if Shiloh could work for him when the war was over.

"I'd miss her, but you treat her good. Much better than the plantation. We'll tell Pa Lou she be real good taken care of."

Though Nashoba had said nothing then, he'd pressed a strong hand onto Philip's shoulder, then the top of his head.

And he said nothing now, knowing instinctively it was not the time to reveal what had been growing inside of him regarding her. Instead, he squeezed her shoulders, then tilted his chin towards the shore when she looked at him.

"Time to go?" she asked. He nodded. "Reckon so..."

She turned her back to him and rinsed off fully. He couldn't keep from gazing at the strong slope of her back to her wonderfully rounded rear and powerful thighs. Nashoba breathed deeply and prayed his body's reaction would dissipate quickly, turning around so he could rinse off as well. With his back to the bank, he heard her wade out of the water onto the shore, but he didn't glance back until he thought enough time had passed for her to dress.

Shiloh was still provocative fully clothed however, much to Nashoba's frustration. Because she hadn't fully dried, the shift she wore molded to her body. He could clearly see the points of her breasts and the outline of the space between her legs, and he had more trouble controlling his body's response now than he'd had when they'd been fully nude with her in his arms. He was mildly annoyed by the way she blithely paced the creek's bank, re-braiding and tying up her hair. She hummed a song Nashoba had taught her, and he suddenly was struck by homesickness so strong he sagged in the water.

"Nashoba!" she called, about to rush in, but he held out a hand to stay her. "You okay?"

He nodded and walked out of the water. She kept her attention to his face, hers so full of her concern, and he framed it in his hands for added reassurance before putting on his loincloth and trousers.

"You sure?" she asked skeptically.

"Do not worry about me, *Chilita*." He took her arm and threaded it through his. Shiloh remained silent but hugged his arm closer to her. When they reached the outer edge of the camp, she rose on her tiptoes and kissed his cheek.

"I always worry about you," she whispered against his skin, then went to her section of the camp.

Nashoba wanted to pulled her back and kiss her properly, but the timing wasn't right. She still considered him a friend; but more than that, Nashoba didn't think she was comfortable enough in her power as a woman.

Yet he couldn't deny he wanted to be the one to teach her how to be.

So instead, he taught her other things—how to wrestle, which herbs were edible, how to fish with a spear, even how to operate a gun, although they couldn't really shoot it because bullets were precious and the reports were too loud. His first lessons were actually on the parts of a gun and how to clean and repair one, which had irritated her because the lessons were, in her words, "boring." But eventually they advanced to how to hold a weapon, how to use her surroundings to her advantage, how to shoot a moving target or while moving herself. He also cautioned her on the power of a gun's recoil, and the importance of the draw.

She was getting exceptionally good at that.

And as much as he knew this would all be much better if they could actually shoot the weapon, he wouldn't risk it. Besides, maybe she *would* come with him after the war was over, and he could definitely teach her properly then...

"I cannot believe you've not tasted her yet!"

Nashoba glared at Koi as they got ready for the night. The heat and humidity that lingered long after the sun set made breechcloths the only acceptable attire for slumber other than nudity. He'd just returned from watching Shiloh and her brothers perform, whistling the last tune they'd played.

"She's not food," he responded in Choctaw.

"That doesn't mean she won't be as delicious as she looks! I heard—"

"Nothing that bears repeating," Nashoba interrupted, pinning him with a hard stare. "You know you sound like the white men who speak of our women so disrespectfully?"

Koi reared back with a scowl at that comparison. "It's not the same—!"

"No? How is it not? I know for a fact we all bleed red. We all have the same parts, same fears, loves, hates. We are no different from the Black man or the white man."

Koi scoffed, but he wasn't nearly as assured as before. "Black men are slaves!"

Nashoba chuckled dryly and settled onto his bedroll. "And so are we."

The battalion started seeing more action than mere patrols and was sent out to battle minor skirmishes that rose up in the area. It took away precious leisure time to spend with Shiloh and he hoped she was finding time to practice without him. Thankfully, there were few injuries or casualties on these outings; but the rumblings throughout camp were the Confederacy was losing significant ground, especially after the defeat in Vicksburg a few months ago.

Another occurrence was more and more Negroes were fleeing. It seemed the majority of them hadn't initially trusted the announcement they were "free" to leave, remembering what the consequences had been before should a slave try to flee and get caught. However, more were growing bolder by the day, yet Shiloh and her brothers still remained.

"So much more to learn and nowhere to go," Shiloh had said when he'd asked her during a knife-throwing lesson. "I got two brothers; I want them to learn as much as they can while here before they go off. Also, we get meals and shelter here. This is the best place to be until we figure out alternatives."

She rarely spoke about herself as a sole character. Every decision she made had her brothers in mind. Nashoba admired that about her. However, he hadn't suggested she and her brothers return with him to Choctaw Nation, uncertain they'd be any freer there than they were here. He didn't think the Union's laws had any bearing on Indian governments—at least he hoped they didn't—and he wouldn't risk their freedom on a maybe. But there was another way he could guarantee it, even if the Choctaws were a matriarchal society.

Did he dare propose marriage? Many unions were built on far less, after all. At least they held mutual regard for one another. Would she even want to learn and live Choctaw ways? Granted, his Nation had melded many European customs into its own, including slavery, but maybe she'd want to be with her people instead?

"We're even more quiet than usual, Nashoba."

He jerked slightly, startled out of his thoughts. It was the middle of the night with a full moon shining above, and he and Shiloh had gone to "their" section of the creek, the lantern Nashoba borrowed adding to the soft moonlight. He looked at her, smoothing his hand along her head. She grinned in return, resting her chin on her raised knees.

"This is no place for you or your brothers, *Kana*. You should do like the other Negroes and leave."

She pursed her lips and looked across the creek. "To where? Everything we know is here."

"North. West. There are opportunities either place, even in the midst of a war."

"We could go back to the plantation! Pa Lou—"

"Thought a war camp would be better for you than it," Nashoba reminded her. "He wants you free from the life he has been forced to live. Would you truly throw his sacrifice, to never see you or your brothers again, back into his face like that?"

There was no immediate response, but the burst of a sob snapped Nashoba's head toward his night companion. Her shoulders bobbed and she tried to fold herself tighter than before. Murmuring Shiloh's name, he settled behind her and enfolded her into his arms. She cried against his arm and he whispered assurances and encouragement in Choctaw. She shifted until they were chest to chest, her face buried in his neck.

"I'm afraid," she whispered. "I feel so lost. What if I ain't strong enough?"

"*Chilita*, do not doubt yourself. If you were a man, you would be right out there on the battlefield!"

"On the other side," she said with humor in her voice.

He laughed and pressed his nose against hers. "Undoubtedly."

Shiloh caressed his jaw. The mirth in her eyes faded away to reveal an emotion Nashoba hoped he wasn't imagining. His arms tightened around her and his breath caught when her lips brushed his.

"Shiloh—"

He cut himself off when she stiffened then turned away from him. He grasped her chin and made her face him again, but she kept her eyes downcast.

"I'm sorry. Just wanted to know what a kiss felt like."

Nashoba closed his eyes and air entered his lungs slowly. He let them burn for a moment, then exhaled, lifting her face so their eyes met.

"That was a brief touch of flesh, not a kiss."

Her shoulders sagged and her lips poked out. "Oh, poot, I did it wrong!"

Smiling gently, Nashoba grazed the pad of his thumb against her bottom lip. "You would like a genuine kiss?"

She nodded. "The women say it's better when it's with someone you like, and I like you, Nashoba. Can I try again? Reckon I shoulda asked you that the first time!"

His smile widened and he pressed it against her forehead, then closed his lips as he descended the bridge of her nose. Shiloh's hand curled against his shoulder when he touched the tip of her nose with his mouth. She began shivering, and he brought her tight against him. Shiloh tilted her face up and he married their lips together without preamble. She sighed into his mouth and he answered with a moan.

Shiloh jerked away. "I hurt you?! I did it wrong again—!"

Nashoba's mouth stole the rest of her off-base assessment. Her fingers dug into his shoulders as she awkwardly returned the kiss. His body began to stir, so he pulled back completely from her. Shiloh regarded him with awe and confusion.

"I'm bad at this, ain't I?"

He laughed at such a ridiculous notion. "If you were any better, I would be inside you now." When her eyes widened, Nashoba shook his head and handed the lantern to her. "You should go, Shiloh."

"But—!"

"Please. You are not safe with me." He shucked off his loincloth and waded into the creek, ignoring Shiloh's calls of otherwise. But one pierced his consciousness and embedded itself into his soul anyway.

"The safest I ever felt is in your arms, Nashoba."

Precarious Plans

June 1870—Choctaw Territory
(Present-day Oklahoma)

It'd become a routine, more like a ritual, actually. Every morning, Shiloh and Nashoba would meet before sunrise for a dip and a quick bath in the creek. They would tell each other what they planned for the day or talk about what problems they were having. Nashoba was surprisingly forthcoming with her; and she hoped, now that she was older, her advice was mature enough for him. That was something she'd missed of Nashoba's friendship—good guidance. It was hard to find a genuine friend, and even more so for that friend to be male. For a single woman, most men only had one aim—to get between her legs. They didn't understand Shiloh wasn't an easy woman, thinking her race and her former status as a slave meant she'd open for anyone. They soon realized it, however, sometimes the hard way. She knew she'd been incredibly blessed to have remained untouched for all those years, but between her former master's policy of no fornication between whites and slaves; the fact her Papa had taught her how to fight and made sure he and her brothers were always around whenever they worked the fields; and the respect most on the plantation had given her Pa Lou, to the point she'd gained a post in the house after her father had been sold, meant there had been little opportunity for such an act to happen. She'd earned an "untouched" status that would've remained until either the master had found a stud for her or Pa Lou had decided a suitor worthy enough; yet, the war had happened before either event could occur.

So now, Shiloh had high standards, even if she weren't the wealthiest or the most beautiful woman in the territory; although when some men became intoxicated, they'd make the latter claim to her. She was rare in her liberation. There was no husband to tell her what to do, no master, no employer. Even the former owner of the Gilded Canary had treated them more like his children than his subordinates. Considering her Philip really had become the son he'd never had, Shiloh was grateful destiny had cleared a path for them towards people who truly cared.

She wasn't entirely sure where Dr. Clinton fit in all of this, and she didn't feel comfortable bringing him up with Nashoba, either. Because of his duties for his Nation and the United States government, his days tended to run well into the night, which meant they only saw each other during their morning baths. Yet Shiloh knew that was a convenient excuse. She was torn for reasons she'd yet found the courage to admit, let alone speak.

The increasingly rising voices broke Shiloh from her musings. Behind her a card game was going in the wrong direction, and she sighed. It was too early for this nonsense.

"Is there a problem, gentlemen?" she called, not even getting up from her mending of the drapes that had been in the windows. When they ignored her, which she *knew* they had because they'd gotten quiet enough to hear her before growing even louder, she sighed again and drew her knife.

"Gentlemen?" she called once more, gritting her teeth when they became even louder. "Enough of this," she muttered under her breath, and threw the knife. It pierced the bills and cards in the center of their table, not even an inch away from the warring hands. All reared back, some people so forcefully they fell back onto the floor in their chairs. Shiloh rolled her eyes and yanked the knife out of the table, disturbing the pile of bills and cards. She glared at every one of them silently and sheathed the knife back into her boot.

"I don't want to have to tell you again," Shiloh warned. They all nodded and dispersed quickly with their cards and shares of money.

Throughout it all, her brothers had kept performing, although Philip was busy trying not to laugh. Shiloh rolled her eyes again but grinned at him while Albert, Mary, and Clarice shook their heads from either relief or chastisement. Shiloh really didn't care; it was her job to keep order around here, and that was what she'd do.

She returned to her mending, focused but never so focused that she lost track of what was going on around her. A few hours after noon, she spotted Dr. Clinton entering, stopping by the bar only for Mary to point in her direction. She returned her eyes to her mending, dropping her feet from the chair she'd had them on since she knew he was coming to join her.

"I hear there was a tussle," Dr. Clinton said, standing by the chair.

"All settled now," Shiloh said, glancing at him. "Would you like to sit?"

Dr. Clinton smiled and did so. "I would also like to escort you to the church's social on Saturday."

The church's social usually occurred the first Saturday after the summer solstice, for it would be the longest Saturday of the year with daylight. Shiloh had been looking forward to spending the day with her family, and especially her daughter who would be old enough to truly enjoy it for the first time. But the element of Dr. Clinton made her feel uneasy. If she went with him, it would all but broadcast the fact he was courting her. Notably, that shouldn't matter since he'd just about walked her home every night ever since that first time, and they would sit on the swinging chair and talk for a spell. Actually, he mostly talked while she listened. He rarely asked her to expand on how her day went; and when she brought it up, he'd deftly change the subject. Her occupation obviously made him uncomfortable, and he would always ask her to visit him while at work.

"I know you did some nursing during the war," he'd tell her. "I think it would be a shame for you not to keep those skills honed."

Shiloh knew he wasn't wrong, but she also knew she wouldn't like that as much as what she did here. Here, she was her own master, had her own life. She didn't want to work *for* anyone else if she didn't have to. She wouldn't be an equal partner with Dr. Clinton, and they both knew that.

"You just want to keep an eye on me," Shiloh said instead, injecting humor into her tone.

"Both eyes, if I could, for you are beautiful, Shiloh."

She smirked a little. She was wearing a blue, flannel shirt and denims with a holster on her belt and a knife tucked in her boot. "Beautiful" wasn't usually the term one used for such an ensemble on a woman.

"You flatter too much," she accused.

"It's only flattery if you don't deserve it. What I speak is truth."

Shiloh couldn't help her smile and she inclined her head to him. "Thank you, Dr. Clinton."

"Lamont. Surely we've moved beyond such formal address."

She nodded again. "Lamont."

Mary came by with a plate of jerky and corn, beaming so brightly at them Shiloh almost shaded her eyes. Lamont laughed softly and blessed his food, then regarded her again.

"Will you let me escort you and Tempest to the social?"

Shiloh finished a stitch and took a deep breath. "All right."

Lamont rapped the wooden table in triumph and nodded. "Great! I will come for you around ten on Saturday."

As usual, Shiloh listened while Lamont spoke about the cases he'd had that morning. During the course of this, her brothers came and greeted him, and she used that as an excuse to take her leave. When she reached the bar and poured herself some water, she shot both Mary and Clarice a quelling look.

"Not a word!" Clarice promised, holding up her hands in surrender.

"I have the *perfect* dress for you, though!" Mary said, and the two women giggled and slapped hands.

Shiloh groaned and dropped her head onto the bar in response. She didn't look up when the women abruptly stopped laughing, either, rolling her forehead along the wood as she gripped the glass of water.

"Long day, *Kana*?"

Shiloh shot up with wide eyes and almost fell off of her stool. A strong hand grasped her waist and kept her upright.

"Na-than!"

His grin was lopsided and his thumb grazed her gently, making her shiver imperceptibly. "I did not mean to startle you."

A glance to her sisters-in-law revealed slack jaws and a borderline indecent amount of lust in their eyes. Shiloh frowned at him and was about to speak when Philip interrupted.

"Hey! Nathan! Goodness!" He came and clapped Nashoba's shoulder. "How are you?"

"You have grown, finally, Philip. Good to see you," Nashoba replied, grasping Philip's shoulder in kind. Albert didn't seem quite as happy to see the man, but he did nod a greeting. "You as well, Albert."

"You all know each other?" Clarice asked, surprise lacing her voice.

"Yeah! He helped us get out of Meridian!" Philip said. "Didn't think we'd ever see you again!"

"I'm sure he thought likewise," Albert deadpanned, folding his arms across his chest. "So that was you the other night, huh? Which was why Shiloh let you walk away uninjured—"

"All right, now," Shiloh chastised, looking up and noticing Lamont approaching. She cursed under her breath and stood to intercept.

"Lamont—"

"Lamont?" Nashoba asked, pulling even with her.

Lamont stepped back, then gave a loud laugh and a slap on his thigh. "Nathan Meeks?! Well, I'll be!"

Shiloh returned to the bar and demanded Mary fix her something a hell of a lot stronger than the water she was having. There were coincidences, and then there was God using one's life for laughs. Shiloh took the whiskey Mary offered and drained it in one gulp.

"More—"

"Hey, wait a second! You shouldn't be drinking like that, *especially* without some food to go with it—!"

"Get me another and a piece of bread!" she said lowly, completely ignoring Lamont.

"He is right, *Kana*; you should not overindulge."

Shiloh huffed and released the empty glass. She stood from the stool, looking at none of the men behind her, and told Mary and Clarice she was going home.

Alone.

"Are you not well?" Lamont asked. "Maybe you should stop by my—"

"*Home!*" Shiloh barely repressed snarling the word. "The saloon can survive without me, can't it?"

Albert's lips were set in a tight line while Philip regarded her with confusion. Mary and Clarice were dazed and the two men who'd sparked the turmoil within her looked at her with so much concern she had to flee. She walked out of the establishment without looking back at anyone, and didn't slow her stride until she reached the steps of the boarding house. She didn't enter, however, instead sitting on those steps and pressing her forehead to her knees.

Shiloh made an *oof!* sound when an unexpected force hit her back, but the giggles and kisses that followed brought a smile to her eyes. Cooing, she swung her daughter into her lap and cuddled her, needing uncomplicated affection in her life right then.

"Something happened at the saloon?" Mama Kay asked.

"Just needed a break. I may go back and close up."

"Nah, just stay here. Tempest will only let you out of her sight once a day, after all," Mama Kay teased with a wink. Tempest laughed and wriggled out of her mother's embrace to frolic in the dusty front yard. Shiloh leaned back on her hands and watched her daughter's vibrant play. Tempest had so much energy, always ready with a smile or a laugh. Currently, Tempest was focused on the ground, which meant she was probably searching for some creepy crawlies. Shiloh shuddered at the thought of what her child might find.

She allowed Tempest to play until close to dusk, and they went to the back so they could rinse off enough for dinner. They then entered the kitchen to help prepare the meal, Shiloh bracing herself for Lamont's arrival. But she almost dropped the bowl of squash when she saw who was in tow.

"I hope you don't mind me bringing a guest!" Lamont said, grinning as he clapped Nashoba's back. "I met him while training to be a doctor in Washington—one of my apprenticing doctor's patients!"

"He'd been the local doctor in Kentucky where I went to college," Nashoba had said with a nod. "When he decided to go to Washington and try his luck there, I went with him and worked for the government."

"It was good because Dr. Hascomb treated the free Blacks in the area; it was a godsend," Lamont declared. His eyes widened with excitement when Mama Kay appeared with a tray of cured ham. "*And* did you know Nathan helped Shiloh and her brothers escape a Confederate camp?"

Mama Kay twirled around with a gasp. "Oh! Then you *must* stay! I'm surprised your brothers and their wives didn't come!"

"Mary thought that was too many extra mouths unannounced," Lamont said with a grin.

Mama Kay squared her shoulders proudly. "I did good with my baby!"

"Yes, ma'am, you did."

"Nathan Meeks," Nashoba introduced himself with a bow of his head.

"You can go on and call me Mama Kay!" she said in return. "Anyone who saved my babies is an automatic member of the family!"

"Mama! I got the cornbread!"

Tiny feet pattered against the plank floors of the house into the dining room. Shiloh bobbled her squash at the sound and whirled around to a pleased Tempest carrying a bread basket and wearing a smile.

"Aren't you a good helper?" Mama Kay asked, taking the bread basket from her. "Shiloh, are you going to put that squash down any time soon? We should hurry up and eat before the food gets cold!"

Though everything looked scrumptious, Shiloh barely touched her food, her appetite leaving as soon as Lamont and Nashoba had entered her home. Thankfully, Mama Kay and Lamont dominated the dinner conversation. Nashoba was seated directly across from her at the table with Lamont while Mama Kay and Mr. Upton sat at the heads, but she had a hard time maintaining eye contact with him. Shiloh did listen intently while Nashoba explained he did work for the United States Government at a nearby outpost to facilitate Indian and United States relations.

Mama Kay humphed and shook her head. "Hear they're losing land, but that's what they get for fighting on the wrong side!"

It was a moment before Nashoba answered. "The Confederacy had made a better offer. It is no different than many slaves siding with the British during the war that secured yo—this nation's independence."

Shiloh did glance at Nashoba then and offered him a smirk that he returned.

She was also able to laugh when Tempest enthusiastically asked for ice cream and bristled when Lamont cautioned her about having too many sweets so close to bedtime. She didn't miss Nashoba's brows furrowing at the chastisement, which compelled Shiloh to declare one heaping scoop a sufficient compromise to Lamont's point and Tempest's wish. When her daughter finished her dessert, Shiloh excused them both to prepare her for bed.

"Goodnight kisses!" Tempest announced, and gave one to Mama Kay, Mr. Upton, who chuckled, and Lamont, per usual before she went to bed. But Shiloh's legs nearly gave out when Tempest yanked her hand out of her mother's grasp to run up to Nashoba and kiss his jaw, as that was the only part of him she could reach even on tiptoe.

"Goodnight, Mista Meeks!" came the innocent salutation as Tempest returned to her mother. Nashoba nodded back as if in a haze, his eyes clashing with Shiloh's. She wondered if the reason he couldn't speak was because his throat was clogged like hers.

Shiloh didn't return downstairs after settling Tempest into bed, too busy staring at her child to do so. She didn't jump at the knock on her door nor turn around when Mama Kay entered. A maternal hand settled upon the top of her head and she leaned against the plump body behind her. For a while they just listened to the soft breathing of the child in the room.

"It's time to leave the past in the past, sweetheart," Mama Kay advised eventually. "Dr. Clinton is your future now. He will provide for you and Tempest well."

Mama Kay kissed the top of Shiloh's head, brushed a finger down Tempest's cheek, then left the room. It was still another hour before Shiloh could fall into a restless sleep.

The next morning when she awoke, she decided to really try with Lamont, especially when Nashoba didn't show up at the creek that predawn.

They portrayed the perfect potential couple at the social that weekend, Shiloh very grateful to Philip and Clarice for occupying Tempest for most of the day. Members of the church's congregation greeted them with smiles and nods, approvals that made Shiloh suffocate. It didn't help Lamont had been a perfect gentleman all day, either. He'd complimented both her and Mary on the dress Mary had chosen for her to wear. He'd complimented Mama Kay on making the best pecan pie he'd ever had. He'd made sure Shiloh hadn't had to lift a finger all afternoon, waiting on her and providing whatever she desired. She'd been doing so well until the gathering suddenly went eerily silent and Lamont stood in the middle of it all. When he looked at her with the softness of cotton in his eyes, Shiloh stood from the blanket she'd been sitting on and fled.

Dare to Go

February, 1864—Meridian, Mississippi

The only thing Nashoba hadn't wished was to wait for the Union troops to come to the town. The white Confederate troops had headed for Alabama to regroup, their commanding officer leaving the Choctaw and other "lesser" members of the regiment to "defend" against the oncoming attack. They'd been tasked with pulling up railroad and patrolling nearby waterways to sabotage the Union's journey, but Nashoba had a different duty.

Getting Shiloh and her brothers out safely.

He'd been anticipating and dreading this moment since he'd started hearing rumors about such a move around the white man's Christmas, and he'd convinced Shiloh, Albert, and Philip that would be the perfect time for them to leave. They would have some protection being part of the Union's camp and the Union would probably pay them for their services, which was more than they got here. He'd noticed Shiloh's grin hadn't been as wide as her brothers when he'd proposed that plan to them, and he'd been paradoxically heartened by that.

Since that kiss on the creek's bank, his heart had become fuller and fuller of one Shiloh Ray. They didn't do much beyond that, although Nashoba allowed her to learn his chest and back with her hands and mouth with great frequency. Even though Shiloh offered the same in return, he knew he wouldn't be able to stop with mere tactile exploration. They would spend many nights by that creek in each other's arms talking about what they wanted out of life, how they would live if the world were perfect for a Native man and a Negro woman. Her desires were the most basic— to lead a life of her own choosing, on her own terms, of her own will. To be reunited with Pa Lou and her father. What she would do, she didn't truly know. She'd been enslaved all of her life, after all. As for Nashoba, he wanted to live a life of peace, also on his own terms, on his Nation's own land, without worrying about his way of life being destroyed by broken treaty after broken treaty. More importantly, he wanted the respect due him, that of an equal being under the same Spirits and God as everyone else.

"We are of like mind, then," Shiloh had murmured, her fingers teasing his mouth. He'd grasped them in his hand and kissed their pads.

"And heart," he'd whispered in return, his spirit lightening when she nodded and kissed where her fingers had been mere moments earlier.

Similar interludes had grown even more infrequent than before with the planning of their escape and training Albert and Philip on how to use knives and spar effectively. He'd explained to Shiloh guns and bullets were expensive and too hard to come by, but a man's might and skill were always present.

"Besides, you will be able to teach them should it come to that," he'd told her with a grin.

She'd seemed pleased by the praise. "You think so?"

He'd cupped her jaw, well aware of her brothers looking at them with interest but not caring. "Yes. I'm certain you and your brothers can make it without me."

"You ain't comin' with us?" Philip had asked, his bottom lip poking out.

"He has his own people," Albert had sniffed. "Ain't got no time for us."

"Al! That's not fair—"

"You can take us with you! We good workers!" Albert had pled, forgetting he was almost a fourteen-year-old boy and hugging Nashoba's arm. "Why can't we go with you?"

Nashoba had placed a paternal hand on Albert's forehead before pulling him into a hug. Not to be left out, Philip had joined the embrace. He'd met Shiloh's eyes over their heads to see her valiantly holding back tears. He'd cleared his throat to speak to them.

"You must live your own lives now. You are given a chance of freedom; you should never turn that down. I have every faith, however, we will meet again after this, you as your own men and woman. Do you understand?" The Rays had nodded and that had been the last time anyone had brought up their separation.

"Here."

Nashoba looked up from the satchel he'd been packing full of commandeered items from around camp that he would give to Shiloh. Koi had a stack of bills in his hands—Union bills. Surprised, Nashoba took it from him.

"'Borrowed' from contraband," Koi said in Choctaw with a shrug. "Just in case they go where they won't take

Confederate money." He knew Nashoba had been saving some money from his pay to help the Rays steal away.

"Thank you, Brother," Nashoba whispered, slipping the bills into the bag. He was almost finished, and then they would slip out of camp toward the Union troops. For the past two days, the Union forces had been bent on Meridian's destruction. Instead of fighting in return, Nashoba had been scouting the area to see where those soldiers had made camp and negotiating with a trustworthy old Union cook about seeing to the Rays' safety. He'd worn civilian clothes to hide the fact he was a Confederate soldier during these escapades, and tonight was the night of the transfer.

"They'll be okay, Nashoba," Koi said firmly. "Have faith in the Spirits and God to guide them."

Nashoba nodded. "I know."

His friend was silent for a moment before asking, "Why don't you just marry her, Nashoba? Anyone who has eyes, and many who don't, can see you love her. She feels the same too."

Nashoba shook his head. "She deserves this chance, Koi. She needs to be among her people, learn how to navigate this new world being free—she and her brothers. They still need her. She's all they have."

"They could have you, too, and us, the Choctaw," Koi insisted.

"Many of us didn't treat slaves any better than the white men did. I'm not doing that to them."

Koi glared at him for a moment, then sighed. "I understand."

"If it's our destiny to be, we will be," Nashoba said quietly as he stood with the fully packed satchel. The men, friends who'd become brothers through battle, clasped forearms in goodbye and good luck. "I shall see you soon."

The Rays were waiting at their predetermined location, his and Shiloh's part of the creek. All three were wearing frayed gray shirts and britches. The one sheet they'd fashioned into a sling full of their combined belongings was slung around Shiloh's body. Albert carried their bedrolls on his back. Shiloh wasn't wearing a coat, having given hers to Philip since he'd outgrown his from last winter. She didn't shiver despite the temperature being close to freezing.

"Are you ready?" Nashoba asked them. The trio nodded.

Though the moon wasn't yet completely full, there was enough light from it to guide the way. Nashoba was point while Shiloh brought up the rear, something Nashoba didn't like but knew had to happen because they were the two most skilled at defending. His Union contact, aptly named Prudence, was to meet them at the tree line around the Union camp at dawn. They were going to reach it well before then, but Nashoba and Shiloh had decided camping out there before then was much better than sleeping in the Confederate camp and waking up early.

No one complained during the journey, and they reached the spot Nashoba had chosen for them much earlier than he'd anticipated. Nashoba built a fire while Shiloh spread out the bedrolls and coaxed her brothers to sleep. Even though there were enough blankets for all three, Albert and Philip opted to share one for warmth.

Shiloh hugged the extra bedroll against her and regarded Nashoba across the fire. "You should stay and get some rest." He'd intended to make sure they were settled before going back to the Confederate camp. He wouldn't be there when Prudence came for them.

"I should leave," he said quietly, mindful of her slumbering brothers. It hadn't taken long for their snores to mingle with the other night sounds. He remembered Shiloh telling him they could both fall asleep in a beat and rest just like logs during the night.

With a wry grin, Shiloh approached him and spread out the roll right next to him. "Stay and sleep. Just for an hour."

He gazed at her and grasped her hand. Shiloh sank to her knees, meeting Nashoba's mouth as he sat up to meet hers. Her arms automatically wrapped around his neck, and he pulled her into his lap. She straddled him, the hardening length of him pressing against her warm center. She released a choked moan against his mouth and broke the kiss with a gasp.

"Stay," she whispered, and he felt her tears against his cheeks.

His smile was wistful. "If this were another time, another reality, I'd go to *chishki*, your mother; *chiki*, your father; and Pa Lou. I'd give *chishki* beads and *chiki* a breechcloth, then speak to your Pa Lou in earnest and pray your parents would take the gifts, for that would mean they approved of me."

Shiloh kissed his cheeks, his nose, his lips. "They would approve. They would, Nashoba, they would!"

"And if we were not at war," he continued, pulling back to look into her teary eyes and wiping the moisture from her face with his thumbs, "I would throw pebbles at you and hope you'd throw them back at me, letting me know you'd be my wife."

She rested her forehead against his. "I would, Nashoba. I'd marry you." He kissed her softly. His hands moved from her neck to her breasts. He palmed her soft globes and she moaned again. "Show me what you'd do on our wedding night," she murmured against his mouth.

He shook his head even as he nibbled her neck. "Do not ask that of me, Shiloh. I cannot guarantee I'll be noble."

Shiloh bit the lobe of his ear and ground against him. "I don't want your nobility, Nashoba. I want your love."

By the Spirits and God, it was already hers, and she was claiming the bounty of his heart. Caught, unable to deny her anything, Nashoba twisted until she was on her back upon the bedroll and he loomed over her. The fire's flames were a dull gold against her dark, glorious face, and he had the sudden need to see her bathed in firelight alone.

Reverently and a little nervously, Nashoba undressed her, not allowing her to assist him. He wanted this privilege alone. Though this wasn't the first time they would see each other unclothed, this was the first time he could convey just how marvelous he thought her to be.

"Tell me if you become too cold," he said on a breath. She nodded and smiled.

The nipples of her full, rounded breasts were black against the dark brown of her skin. They compelled him to suckle them like a babe, and the heartbreaking image of their child doing the same flit through his mind. In another time, it would be their future, but not this one.

She held him close and opened her legs as he pushed down her britches, though not all the way off. He kissed his way up her throat to her mouth while his hands found the soaked space between her thighs. His length hardened even more, anxious to be inside of her, but he had to prepare her properly.

As his mouth loved her face, he slipped first one finger, then two inside of her, pleased when her hips quickly found the rhythm he'd set. Her pants were breathless and intoxicating, her arms banding around his neck to bring him closer.

"Nash—Na—*please*, oh, *please!*" she moaned into his neck. Her wet channel fluttered around his fingers. He muffled his groan against her hair and shoved his breeches down his hips to his knees. She reached between them and grasped his erection, then began to stroke. He covered her hand with his to apply the right rhythm and pressure. Her hand was a searing, soft glove dangerously close to bringing him to the brink too soon.

"I have to be inside of you now, Shiloh," he told her against her lips. "Open for me, *Haloka*."

She did, whimpering when the head of him brushed the core of her. He melded their lips together as he joined his body with hers. The pain at his entrance sent shock through her body and a woeful moan escaped, but his hands and whispered assurances soothed away the discomfort. She was so wet and tight around him, clinging as if she'd never let go. He didn't want to leave, either.

"You're inside me, Nashoba," she said into his cheek. "You feel so good, so full!" She laughed and pulled back. "No wonder the women in camp went off to the woods with their lovers!"

He smiled and nipped her nose. "It'll get even better."

He began to stroke deeply, firmly. Her eyes would widen with each penetration, his name a mere exhalation. She wrapped herself tighter around him, barely giving him room to maneuver, so he entered her as deeply as he could go, then twirled his hips. She started to gasp and shudder, her nails digging into his back, and his own release wasn't far behind.

"Nash—*oh!*" She groaned loudly, and his lips fell upon hers to keep her as quiet as possible and to muffle his own shout as he emptied himself inside of her. He collapsed atop her, his heart racing in his chest, her breath warm against his jaw.

She caressed the damp tendrils of the hair along his temple and the nape of his neck. She also smelled of perspiration and their union.

"Maybe I'll take you up on that offer for rest," Nashoba said once he was sure he had a proper breath.

Shiloh palmed his face and dragged her nose against his. "Good."

Nashoba tore off the bottom of his shirt to use as a cloth to cleanse Shiloh of their fluids. When they were fully clothed again, he stood and brought the other bedroll next to the one she'd given him and told her to lie down.

"I may not be here when you awake," he warned her as he tucked her in. "I have to be back before dawn."

She nodded in understanding but smiled. "You'll always be with me."

He kissed her forehead. "So will you, *Haloka*."

Nashoba sat next to her and held her hand while she fell asleep. When her breaths became deep and even, Nashoba cleaned the other bedroll as best he could, then checked on Albert and Philip before stepping back to Shiloh. He kissed her lips chastely and whispered a prayer for her and her brothers. He then left them and his heart to return to the Confederate camp.

Where You Belong

July 1870—Choctaw Territory

(Present-day Oklahoma)

There was a light thump against Shiloh's shoulder, and she twisted all around to see from where it could've possibly come before looking down to determine what it was. A smooth, milky pebble rested behind her, and she frowned at it until another similar sensation occurred on her other shoulder. This pebble was pinkish in color, and she glared at it in utter confusion. She picked up both stones warily.

"What in the world—?"

"Mama! I was *so* close!" Tempest announced with a pout, her fishing spear high over her head in outrage over the naked point of it.

"Try again, dear one," Shiloh insisted, one hand on her knife that she'd been using to gut the fish. They already had plenty for the Fourth of July fish fry that would take place that evening, but Tempest wanted to try to catch a few on her own. Shiloh didn't mind the extra time at the creek herself; she liked the peace.

Ever since she'd run out on Lamont at the church's social, whispers had followed her wherever she went. She did have a long talk with Lamont when she'd finally returned from hiding out at the creek that evening; he'd been waiting for her on the porch with a smoking pipe in his hand. She told him everything about Nashoba, from befriending him at the Confederate camp to his helping her and her family escape. She hadn't seen him in six years, and he'd reentered her life about the same time Lamont had.

"Too much too soon?" Lamont had asked rhetorically. "Or too little, too late?"

"Lamont—"

He'd smiled faintly and held up his hand. "A little of both, I wager." He'd stood and sighed. "You need to resolve whatever it is between you two, Shiloh. I wouldn't want you to treat some other man how you treated me."

She'd winced at that. "I'm sorry, Lamont."

"Yeah, I am too," he'd said, then gone into the house.

Despite his humiliation at the social, Lamont was never cruel to her in public. Though he'd returned to the hotel and no longer sat in the row with Mama Kay or the rest at church, he still greeted them all politely and patronized the Gilded Canary. He also began courting the banker's daughter, a far more appropriate choice for such a man as he. She wouldn't be surprised if he announced their engagement at tonight's fish fry.

Mama Kay and Mary bemoaned the failed suit and foretold doom and gloom for Shiloh, while Albert threatened to put a bullet through Nashoba's head the next time he saw him. Shiloh tried to tell them what had happened between her and Lamont would've happened even if there were no Nashoba, but they didn't believe her. However, Philip and Clarice supported her decision.

"We'll help you," Philip had said one night while they were closing the Canary. "Should you ever need it, Shiloh. You've done so much for us. We owe you at least that!"

She smiled at that memory, and at her daughter throwing her stick into the water in frustration before folding her arms at her chest with a furious scowl.

"Patience, *Haloka*; let the fish come to you."

Both she and her daughter regarded the owner of the new voice. Nashoba was just out of the trees wearing only his breeches. His feet were bare and his brown hair blew in the light breeze of the early morning. She was surprised to see him; he hadn't come to the creek since the evening of the dinner at the boardinghouse.

"May I show you, *Saso Tek*?" he asked, looking at Tempest. She nodded, grabbing the stick from where it floated before her. Nashoba walked to the creek's bank, then abruptly turned and came to Shiloh instead.

"Do you mind if I teach our daughter how to fish, *Haloka*?" Shiloh dropped her head and began to cry. Nashoba lifted her face and kissed away her tears.

"Is that what *saso tek* means?" she asked. "Daughter?" Nashoba nodded. "And *haloka*?"

"Beloved."

She hugged Nashoba close.

"I am sorry to be so delayed, but I had to make arrangements within the Nation so you and Tempest would be recognized as members."

"Why are you so certain Tempest is yours?" she asked.

Instead of being offended, Nashoba smiled. "She is the right age; she has my mother's eyes." He nuzzled her nose. "And she is a dream come true."

For the next hour, Nashoba taught his child how to spear a fish. Tempest caught two on her own, and her parents applauded her accomplishment. When the lesson ended, Tempest had no qualms about allowing Nashoba to hold her when they returned to the creek's banks, nor did she leave her father when he sat next to Shiloh. Nashoba handed her the new fish they'd caught for gutting; but otherwise, there was silence between the three of them.

Until Shiloh threw the pebbles back at Nashoba's head. He, his new fiancée, and their daughter laughed long and loud at that.

SJF

SAVANNAH J. FRIERSON

Originally from Blythewood, SC, Savannah J. Frierson has been writing since she was twelve years old, releasing her debut novel *Being Plumville* in March 2007 with iUniverse, Inc. She has released more publications since then, and they are available at all online book retailers or by request at brick and mortar bookstores. For more information about other titles, please visit Savannah's Web site at http://www.sjfbooks.com or contact Savannah by e-mail at me@sjfbooks.com.

BcccD 11/18

CPSIA information can be obtained
at www.ICGtesting.com
Printed in the USA
LVHW05s1600270718
585151LV00010B/652/P